My First Mother Goose Book

Illustrated by Aurelius Battaglia

Golden Press • New York

Western Publishing Company, Inc., Racine, Wisconsin

Copyright © 1980 by Western Publishing Company, Inc. All rights reserved.
Printed in the U.S.A.
No part of this book may be reproduced or copied in any form without
written permission from the publisher.
GOLDEN®, A GOLDEN STORYTIME BOOK, and GOLDEN PRESS® are trademarks of
Western Publishing Company, Inc.
Library of Congress Catalog Card Number: 80-50140
ISBN 0-307-11987-4

DEFGHIJ

Mary had a little lamb,
　Its fleece was white as snow;
And everywhere that Mary went
　The lamb was sure to go.

Baa, baa, black sheep, have you any wool?
Yes, sir, yes, sir, three bags full.
One for my master,
And one for my dame,
And one for the little boy
Who lives down the lane.

Little Bo-Peep has lost her sheep,
  And can't tell where to find them.
Leave them alone, and they'll come home,
  Wagging their tails behind them.

Simple Simon met a pieman,
    Going to the fair;
Says Simple Simon to the pieman,
    "Let me taste your ware."

Says the pieman to Simple Simon,
    "Show me first your penny."
Says Simple Simon to the pieman,
    "Indeed I have not any."

Hot cross buns!
Hot cross buns!
One a penny, two a penny,
Hot cross buns!

If your daughters do not like them,
Give them to your sons;
One a penny, two a penny,
Hot cross buns!

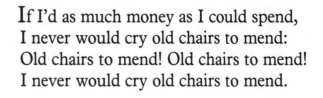

If I'd as much money as I could spend,
I never would cry old chairs to mend:
Old chairs to mend! Old chairs to mend!
I never would cry old chairs to mend.

Sing a song of sixpence,
A pocket full of rye;
Four and twenty blackbirds
Baked in a pie!

When the pie was opened,
The birds began to sing;
Wasn't that a dainty dish
To set before the king?

The king was in his counting-house,
Counting out his money;

The queen was in the parlor,
Eating bread and honey.

The maid was in the garden,
Hanging out the clothes;
There came a little blackbird,
And snapped off her nose.

One misty, moisty morning,
When cloudy was the weather,
I chanced to meet an old man,
Clothed all in leather.
He began to compliment
And I began to grin.
How do you do, and how do you do,
And how do you do again?

Doctor Foster went to Glo'ster
In a shower of rain;
He stepped in a puddle,
Right up to his middle,
And never went there again.

It's raining, it's pouring,
The old man is snoring;
He went to bed with a cold in his head
And he didn't wake up until morning.

Elsie Marley has grown so fine,
She won't get up to feed the swine,
But lies in bed till eight or nine;
Lazy Elsie Marley.

A diller, a dollar,
A ten o'clock scholar,
What makes you come so soo͟
You used to come at ten o'clo͟
But now you come at noon.

Molly, my sister, and I fell out,
And what do you think it was all about?
She loved coffee and I loved tea,
And that was the reason we could not agree.

There was a little girl,
    and she had a little curl
Right in the middle
    of her forehead;
When she was good,
    she was very, very good,
But when she was bad,
    she was horrid.

To market, to market, to buy a fat pig,
Home again, home again, jiggety-jig;
To market, to market, to buy a fat hog,
Home again, home again, jiggety-jog.

Ride a cock-horse to Banbury Cross,
To see a fine lady upon a white horse;
Rings on her fingers and bells on her toes,
And she shall have music wherever she goes.

Jack and Jill went up the hill,
To fetch a pail of water;
Jack fell down and broke his crown,
And Jill came tumbling after.

See-saw, Margery Daw,
Jack shall have a new master;
Jack shall have but a penny a day,
Because he can't work any faster.

Pease porridge hot,
Pease porridge cold,
Pease porridge in the pot,
Nine days old.

Some like it hot,
Some like it cold,
Some like it in the pot,
Nine days old.

Pat-a-cake, pat-a-cake, baker's man,
Bake me a cake as fast as you can;
Pat it and prick it, and mark it with B,
And put it in the oven for baby and me.

Jack be nimble,
Jack be quick,
Jack jump over the candlestick.

Little Miss Muffet
Sat on a tuffet,
Eating her curds and whey;
Along came a spider,
Who sat down beside her,
And frightened Miss Muffet away.

Little Jack Horner
Sat in the corner,
Eating a Christmas pie;
He put in his thumb,
And pulled out a plum,
And said, "What a good boy am I!"

Hickory, dickory, dock,
The mouse ran up the clock,
The clock struck one,
The mouse ran down,
Hickory, dickory, dock.

Pussy cat, pussy cat, where have you been?
I've been to London to look at the queen.
Pussy cat, pussy cat, what did you there?
I frightened a little mouse under her chair.

Polly put the kettle on,
Polly put the kettle on,
Polly put the kettle on,
  We'll all have tea.

Sukey take it off again,
Sukey take it off again,
Sukey take it off again,
  They've all gone away.

Puss came dancing out of the barn
With a pair of bagpipes under her arm;
She could sing nothing but "Fiddle-de-dee,
The mouse has married the bumblebee."
Pipe, cat; dance, mouse;
We'll have a wedding at our good house.

Go to bed, Tom,
Go to bed, Tom,
Tired or not,
Go to bed, Tom.

Diddle, diddle, dumpling, my son John,
Went to bed with his trousers on;
One shoe off, and one shoe on,
Diddle, diddle, dumpling, my son John.